A Year Full of Holidays

Susan Middleton Elya

illustrated by Diana Cain Bluthenthal

SCHOLASTIC INC.
New York Toronto London Auckland
Sydney Mexico City New Delhi Hong Kong

ISBN 978-0-545-38795-8

12 11 10 9 8 7 6 5 4 3 2 1   11 12 13 14 15 16/0

Printed in the U.S.A.   40

First Scholastic printing, September 2011

Design by Ryan Thomann
Text set in Farao

When Nell had her birthday, her whole house was buzzin'
with family and neighbors and friends by the dozen.

"I love all my presents, and look at this cake!
I have a good wish that I can't wait to make!"

That night, she asked, "When'll my birthday come back?"
"The **holidays**," said Mom, "will help you keep track.

There's one every month, except sometimes there's two.
They'll help pass the time between birthdays for you!"

A whole week went by. Nell needed to know—
was a holiday coming? "Time's moving so slow!"

"You're home on a Monday?"
"**Labor Day**," her dad said,
"when workers can rest and sleep late in bed."

"But we're wide-awake, so what can we do?"

Her dad lit the coals. "Have a big barbecue!"

The first day of school, she said to her friend,
"I hope there's more fun and the holidays won't end."

"That's silly," said Tommy. "The best day I've seen
is coming next month, and it's called **Halloween**!"

When Nell got dressed up,
trick-or-treated 'round town,
she saw gobs of witches,
six ghosts, and a clown.

With her treat bag in tow,
she exclaimed, "This is living!"
"There's more," Tommy added.
"Just wait till **Thanksgiving**."

Then, four Thursdays later, she smelled Grandma's pies—

fresh apple and pumpkin and Mincemeat Surprise!

The next day, her family went down to the mall.
They needed to park but found no spots at all!

When finally they swarmed
through the big, bustling crowd,
"**Christmas** is coming!"
Nell shouted too loud.

And then, the next month, as she counted each day,
young Nell had her mind on a man in a sleigh.

She hung up the stockings,
left cookies and milk,
then wished for some toys
and a kitten like silk.

JANUARY

Then, one week later, a holiday at night!

"I have to skip bedtime."

Her dad said, "All right."

She drank juice so bubbly,
ate **New Year's** spaghetti,
then threw shiny streamers and colored confetti.

Then six long weeks passed.
Now what could be coming?
Her mom fixed her hairdo
and went around humming.

She handed her paper and scissors and lace.
Nell glued decorations all over the place.

A day filled with kisses,
and a flower bouquet,
and candy with words,
all for **Valentine's Day**.

And then, one March morning, when winter was old,
Saint Patrick's Day danced in with rainbows and gold.

So Nell dressed in green, drew some fat Irish clover,
and asked, "May I please have some leprechauns over?"

A few weekends later, Nell said, "Mom, it's funny,
I remember a day with a gift-giving bunny."

She helped dye some eggs, her family's spring habit,
and left out her basket for a sneaky old rabbit.

As she munched **Easter** candy and picked off pink grass,
she asked the new kid in her story-time class,

"Which holiday's next? I hope there's another."
"Of course," said the girl. "It's a day for your mother."

"It's **Mother's Day** Sunday!" She picked a corsage
and made a big card for a free Nell massage.

In place of Mom cooking, Nell did it instead.
She loaded the tray, served her breakfast in bed.

"Is only one holiday happening in May?"

"No," Father said. "There's **Memorial Day**."

They hung up their flag. Some fighter jets flew.

They honored Nell's grandpa with red, white, and blue.

He showed Nell some medals he'd earned in the war.

"They're so shiny," she said. "Do you have any more?"

In June, her mom said,
"**Father's Day** comes up next."
So Nell drew a picture—
with Dad's muscles flexed!

She got out a bucket, said, "Stay where you are."

While Dad read the paper, she washed his whole car.

Next, a parade on the **4th of July**!

She liked all the fire trucks and floats that went by.

When Dad said, "Sit down, Nell,"

she said, "In a minute."

Instead of just watching, she tried to be in it.

Later, her family hiked up to the park.

The fireworks display began after dark.

In August they camped for a very fun week
of pine trees and fireflies and baths in the creek.

And finally—her **birthday**! What wish would she make?
She took a deep breath and blew out her cake.

"I wish time went faster,
and the holidays came quicker,
that the presents were bigger,
and the frosting was thicker!"

It wasn't too long before one part came true.
They all stayed home Monday for a big barbecue!